The
EVIL
WITHIN

CATHERINE MacPHAIL

The
EVIL
WITHIN

INSPIRED BY
THE STRANGE CASE OF DR JEKYLL AND MR HYDE
BY ROBERT LOUIS STEVENSON

Barrington Stoke

First published in 2017 in Great Britain by
Barrington Stoke Ltd
18 Walker Street, Edinburgh, EH3 7LP

www.barringtonstoke.co.uk

Text © 2017 Catherine MacPhail
Illustration © 2017 Barrington Stoke
Illustration by Dominik Nawrocki

A CIP catalogue record for this book is available
from the British Library upon request

ISBN: 978-1-78112-587-8

Printed in China by Leo

Contents

From the journal of Henry Jekyll, aged 14

Edinburgh, 1850

- 1 -

"A Fine Bogey Tale"- Strange Beginnings

The creature loped along the cobbled streets of
the Old Town, darting between shadows, a thing
of the dark. A cat was sheltering in a doorway
when it caught sight of the creature and leaped
to its feet. Its fur stood on end. It arched its back
in anger, and in fear. It hissed as the creature
reached out a hand with long, dirty fingernails to
grab it. The cat was too fast tonight. It skidded
on wet cobbles and disappeared into the foggy
darkness.

The creature moved on.

A light appeared in a narrow window as a
tattered curtain was drawn aside. A woman

looked out. The creature didn't hide. There was nothing for it to be afraid of. Its bold eyes moved to where the woman stood. She held her candle closer to the window and peered out into the gloom of the old close. Her eyes grew wide with fear, her mouth opened and she screamed.

"It's here! The monster is here again."

Candles appeared in other windows, other faces looked out. By then the creature had moved on, a dark shadow flitting fast along the narrow streets.

No one doubted the woman. Too many had seen that same creature on other nights to doubt her. It was hard to say if it was human. Its shadowy form was too twisted to be sure, but many had seen it creep along in the darkness, bent and twisted, like a creature out of a nightmare.

As the woman screamed the cry went up from street to street.

"The Beast is among us!"

☽

"It was a monster," she says, "with fangs and claws and everything."

Our young maid Mary Cole has come home with the story, and now she stands in the kitchen telling it to Mrs Kerr the cook with glee.

"But when the men went searching for it ..." Mary snaps her fingers. "It was gone. Disappeared into the fog, like a spirit. The Old Town is alive with talk of it."

"You said yesterday it was like an ape, with long arms dragging on the ground," Mrs Kerr reminds her.

"I've not seen it myself," Mary says, for she is an honest girl. "I'm just telling you what other people have seen." She pauses for a moment. "But if it is a monster, maybe it can change its shape. Become anything it wants. An ape, a wolf, anything. And everyone agrees on one thing ..."

Mary pauses again. She is truthful but she knows how to tell a story. Her tales bring the creature to life, here in our warm kitchen. "It isn't quite human," she says at last.

Mrs Kerr shakes her head and smiles. She likes Mary. Everyone does.

"You and your wild stories, Mary," she says. "You know the young master has terrible nightmares about this thing that's supposed to be roaming the Old Town."

Mary breaks in. "There's no 'supposed to be' about it, Mrs Kerr," she says. "It *is* wandering the streets ... hunting its prey."

Now Mary has gone too far. Mrs Kerr gives her an angry look. "The mistress does not want anyone talking about it," she says. "Not in this house."

Mary turns back to the dirty dishes. "I won't say another word about it then, Mrs Kerr," she says. "My lips are sewn closed like a corpse's shroud."

Mrs Kerr laughs. "I know you too well, Mary Cole," she says. "An iron bolt welded across your mouth wouldn't shut you up for long." Then she grows serious. "But no more talk of this creature who walks the dark streets, not in this house. We do not want the young master to hear of it."

But the young master has already heard.

I have been standing hidden, listening at the kitchen door. I want to hear the stories of this 'creature', as they call it, this Beast, this monster, this not-quite-human thing. Even if in the night these stories bring me nothing but terror.

☽

I wake up screaming, again. Sweat soaks my nightshirt and my sheets. In that moment between sleep and waking I am still half in the nightmare, half out. Something was chasing me. When I looked behind I could see nothing in the darkness, but I could hear pounding footsteps coming closer.

I shake myself awake, and look around my room to make sure I am home, safe. Early-morning light peeks round the heavy curtains at my window. My room is as it always is, my dresser is in the corner, the mirror is on the wall. I can see my own face in it. How afraid I look, sitting up, my face pale and thin. I tell myself over and over that I am home. I am safe. But, for all I know this, I cannot shake the terror I felt in that dream. The terror that someone was after me, that some strange creature was at my heels, almost upon me.

Then my heart sinks as I realise there was something else, some other terror I couldn't face. But what was it? The nightmare is never clear. Just as I am about to remember, the memory is snatched from me, like a scrap of paper blown away by a sudden wind.

My mother has heard my screams and comes running into my room. She draws back the red velvet curtains, and the grey light of an Edinburgh morning seeps into the room.

"Harry, Harry." She comes and folds her arms around me to comfort me. "You're safe now. Safe at home." I lay my head on her shoulder. "It was only a dream, Harry," she says. "One of your nightmares."

How tired she must be of finding me, awake and shaking, but with no real memory of what has scared me.

"I'm sorry, Mother," I say.

She tuts. "It's not your fault – you have nothing to be sorry for. It's that silly girl, Mary. She's always carrying stories here from the Old Town. I've warned her before. I will dismiss her this time."

"No." I sit up and grip her soft hands. "You mustn't do that, Mother. You can't blame Mary. It's my fault."

It is true. I listen to Mary's stories even when I know they are no good for me. I cannot get them out of my mind. They affect me so. I have too much imagination, my mother says. But how could I not listen? These stories are wonderful for a boy and I cannot resist.

By day, the stories thrill me, fill me with such a sense of adventure. I see myself as the hero who would be the one to find the monster. The only one brave enough to challenge him. In my mind's eye I see myself run after him into the fog. I am on his heels, almost upon him. I trap him in one of the dark closes. He tries to escape, but I battle him with my bare hands, and I win. I am a hero, the one who saves my city.

But then it is night, and darkness falls, and I have no control over my dreams. Then it is only terror I feel when I think of the strange creature in the Old Town. In my dreams, I do not chase him. In my dreams, he chases me. There is something else too, some feeling I cannot quite understand. Try as I might to remember it, that feeling is always gone as soon as I wake, before I can catch hold of it.

"This time I won't dismiss her," my mother says, as if she is granting Mary a pardon. But I know she would never dismiss Mary. Like Mrs

Kerr, she likes her too much. "I wish she was not such a chatterbox," my mother says as she stands and smooths her skirts.

After Mother has gone, I get up from my bed and stand on my stone terrace to breathe in the morning air. I love that my bedroom has this terrace that looks onto our walled garden with the fountain hidden among the flowers. No one can see me here. I am invisible, all alone, yet still in the heart of this splendid city. If only I could banish the nightmares, I would be so very happy.

- 2 -

Weird Tales of the City

"More nightmares," my father says. He sounds disappointed. "How can it be that your dreams are so troubled, my boy?"

My mother has told him. "I can keep nothing from your father," she says with a fond smile at him.

They made a good match, my father and mother. My mother's family considered that she had married beneath her because she is a wealthy woman in her own right. But their love and respect for each other was always clear to see.

My mother's eyes nearly always have a smile in them, while my father is a stern man who is known for being both strict and fair. He stands tall and straight and is always smartly dressed, his whiskers streaked with grey. He is a much-respected doctor, but to me he has only ever been a loving father. He hides it well, but I know my night terrors trouble him almost as much as they do my mother.

We are in the dining room eating breakfast.

"It's all the tales he keeps hearing about this creature in the streets," my mother says. "No wonder he has nightmares. Are the police doing nothing about it?"

"Tales have always been told in Edinburgh, my dear," my father says, in an attempt to soothe her. "Remember, this is the city where not so long ago bodies were snatched fresh from their graves – and worse – to be sold to doctors, such as myself."

My father speaks of the grave robbers who sold still-warm corpses to doctors to study at the university. I had thrilled at stories of grave robbers in the midnight dark of a graveyard, digging up coffins, throwing fresh corpses onto carts and wheeling their sinister cargo along the streets. But Father also hints at the story of Burke and Hare. These two had been greedy, with a lust for blood, and they had no taste for digging. Instead they made their money by murder – selling the bodies of their victims to Dr Robert Knox. We even sang a song in the schoolyard about their dastardly deeds.

Up the close and down the stair,
But and ben with Burke and Hare.
Burke's the butcher, Hare's the thief,
Knox the boy who buys the beef.

Of course, the story of Burke and Hare is not the only weird tale told in this city.

"Don't forget Mary King's Close, Father," I remind him. "The place where Plague victims were sealed up to stop the spread of the deathly disease. They screamed and hammered at the walls to be let out, but the citizens ignored their cries. Those cries became fainter and weaker till at last they all fell silent."

"Yes indeed," my father says.

"They say you can still hear their ghosts cry as they pound on the walls, trying to escape," I say.

"Ah yes, and Burke and Hare still wander the streets looking for their next victim." My father smiles and shakes his head. "We are always eager to create legends and ghost stories from real-life tragedies."

"Thank goodness that is all in the past." My mother shivers as she speaks. Unlike my father and me, she does not relish these strange tales.

"Then there was Deacon Brodie ..." I urge my father on, because this tale is my most favourite.

"No more," my mother says, and she waves her hands to stop my father. But my father, like me, loves the sinister and he goes on.

"Ah yes, Deacon Brodie. Greatly respected member of Edinburgh society, skilful cabinet maker and member of the Town Council ..."

"And, by night, leader of a gang of thieves," I say.

"Indeed. Deacon Brodie led a double life."

A double life. I thrill at the thought. It's an idea that has always fascinated me. What a way to live.

"They say he was hanged on a wooden gibbet of his own making," my father finishes.

"Enough!" For once my gentle mother raises her voice. "We are at table!"

I know all these stories. I have loved listening to every one of them since I was small, yet they never caused me any nightmares. My nightmares only started when the rumours of this dark creature of the shadows began to spread.

My mother fans herself. "I don't want to hear any more," she declares. "Body snatching, corpses dug up from their graves and the spirits of Plague victims stalking the streets. I will be the one having nightmares next." She frowns at my father. "I don't like it here. This city is not a good place for Harry."

"Edinburgh is a city like any other," my father says. "But it is one made for tales of mystery and darkness. Nothing will change that."

I think that my mother is wrong. This is a good place for me. I love Edinburgh. I love how the Castle looms over the whole city. I imagine it standing above us, watching over us, guarding us. I love to walk along the cobbled streets of the Old Town, then head up the Royal Mile that leads to the Castle. I love the sight of Princes Street and the New Town beyond, with its fine houses and elegant streets. When we first moved here I explored for days on end. I walked everywhere in the fierce wind with my mouth open in wonder at my new home's beauty and magic.

I saw how the city seemed to be made up of two parts, two selves, two souls. There were the dark, narrow closes of the Old Town, with its murky past, and the bright light buildings of the New Town, where the streets were clean and wide and fresh. Two completely different places, standing cheek by jowl in the same city.

And, of course, I love the sinister stories of the city. Every close and wynd has one to tell, of plague and murder and body snatching. What 14-year-old boy wouldn't be eager to hear more?

I was never afraid. Not until this strange creature began to walk the night streets. No one caught more than a glimpse as it disappeared into the shadows, misshapen, deformed. Half human, some said. And, for reasons I cannot explain, my nightmares had begun. It puzzled my father too. I knew it.

"Harry was never afraid of anything before this," he would say. "If I remember, he was the one who made others afraid. I had to scold him for putting the fear of death into our maids when he was younger."

I blushed as I remembered how wild I had been. I had placed a grass snake in the old cook's bed that had sent her screaming off into the night, and into someone else's service. "A devil of a boy," she had called me. And then I would wander the house at night, making odd wailing sounds, pretending to be the family ghost. I had such fun watching from the shadows as the maids ran from their rooms in alarm. My father had caught me one night, draped in a sheet, my face white with flour, my hair standing on end.

"The way you behave is not worthy of you, Harry," he said, and he was more angry than I had ever seen him. "It must stop."

If my tricks were cruel they were never meant to be. I enjoyed the mischief I caused, but I knew to obey my father too. And so I sank that side of my nature deep inside me, buried like treasure.

My mother is always ready to take my side. "Ah, but he was only a boy then," she says.

"And almost a man now," my father says. "Is that not right, Harry?"

"You are right, Father, but still …"

My mother shakes her head. "It's this city, it unsettles me with its damp and its dark. I wish we could move."

"Bad things happen everywhere, my dear." My father pats her arm to comfort her. "You remember Inverness, where I had my practice three years ago –?"

"What happened in Inverness?" I ask. Why have I not heard of this before?

"I'm surprised you can't remember, Harry," my father tells me. "A creature was attacking the animals. They thought at first it was a wolf."

"You had nightmares then too," my mother says. "I'm glad you can't remember."

I hardly listen to her words. "You say, *at first*? So it wasn't a wolf?"

"No, it was some young ragamuffins from a village near by. They always denied it – but their guilt was as clear as day. The attacks stopped as soon as they were caught."

"Harry will have more nightmares tonight with all this talk," my mother says.

"No, he will not," my father says. "I shall prepare a sleeping tonic for him."

"No, Father," I protest. "There is no need for anything like that." I had no trouble falling asleep. It's what happened while I slept that made me fearful.

As if he is reading my mind my father says, "With this tonic, your sleep will be sound and unbroken. There will be no dreams."

"Oh please, Harry," my mother pleads. "Take it. You need a good night's rest."

Perhaps she's right. I have had too many nights broken by nightmares. I am always so tired. To sleep without dreams. I pray for such a night.

Tonight I will take the sleeping tonic my father makes me.

- 3 -

Dreamless Sleep

"You're looking well, master," Mary says as I step out of the front door and into the morning air.

She is scrubbing the front steps. I know that my mother frowns upon Mary addressing her 'betters'. Mary knows this too, but she is not one to obey rules. I have a feeling she is not one for thinking anyone is better than she is either. She is the same age as I am, fourteen, and she has been working for us since we moved into our Edinburgh house. She begins long before I am awake. She walks from her home in the Old Town in the winter darkness each morning. When she finishes at night it is dark again and she must walk back along those same narrow streets.

My mother has offered Mary lodgings in the house. She worries about a girl so young walking home alone. But Mary told her, with no hint of self-pity, that she has to be home each night to help her mother with 'the bairns'. Mary has seven younger brothers and sisters, as she told us one day with pride.

"They're all alive and well, sir," she said to my father when he asked about them. This was indeed a thing to be glad of. So many children and infants died before they could grow up.

"We're made of strong stuff, my father says," Mary declared, and the cook scolded her for her boldness.

But my father laughed. "And you're right to be proud of that, Mary. In my work as doctor to the families of the Old Town, I see too many babies taken far too young."

So, this morning, I am not offended or upset by Mary's greeting. I like her, and I know of no one who does not. The sleeping tonic has worked. I have spent the last three nights in deep, dreamless sleep.

"I'm feeling very good, Mary," I tell her.

"And I'm feeling very well too, sir," Mary says. "I think that's because there's been no more sightings of the –" Her hand flies to her mouth as if she could push the words back inside. She looks around in case Mrs Kerr is watching. "Oh, I shouldn't be saying, sir," she mumbles.

"Nonsense," I tell her. "It sounds as if you are spreading good news. And what harm is there in that?" I breathe in the fresh morning air. "So tell me. I long to know. You were saying ... no more sightings ...?"

Mary sits back on her heels and looks right up at me. "No more sightings of the Beast, sir. The monster has left and he will never come back." She speaks as if she knows this without doubt.

"Let us pray that you are right, Mary."

"Oh I do, sir, every night I pray." She clasps her hands together and looks up to the blue skies of the heavens. "I pray he will never come back."

- 4 -

Nothing Human

Dusk had fallen in the Old Town, and candles glowed golden in every window. The streets were almost empty. Music floated on the breeze out of the inns and into the streets – fiddles, and voices lifted in song. People felt safer now. Now that it appeared that the Beast was gone.

If a Beast had ever been in the city at all, some said. For now some believed that the Beast had only been a figment of a drunken imagination. After all, why had the Beast never been spotted in the New Town, with its grand, wide streets and its fine ladies and gentlemen? Why only here, in the Old Town with its common working people, its taverns, its dirt and its drunkenness?

Over the past few nights, the people of the Old Town had relaxed as their fears melted away.

Now, Hannah Byrne stumbled from the warm glow of an Old Town tavern with her friends. It was her birthday and she was celebrating. Eighteen today, and still without a young man. If she didn't hurry up and get one soon, her friends told her, she would end up an old maid. But they laughed as they said it. They were good friends to her. But now, Hannah was tired.

"I have to go home," she said with a giggle. "I have to work in the morning." It was an early start at the paper mill in Dalry and Hannah knew that she'd have a long, hard day ahead.

Hannah's friends wanted to move on to the next tavern. And from there to the next, no doubt – there were many inns and taverns in the Old Town.

"One more drink," they said. "Come on, Hannah, don't be an old maid just yet. What harm will another tot of gin do?"

Hannah shook her head, but that only made her dizzy. She wasn't used to so much drink and she didn't want to get used to it. Now, she just wanted home to the warm bed she shared with her little sister Isobel.

"We can't let you go alone," her friends said.

"But I have nothing to fear," Hannah said. "The streets are safe, and I don't have far to go."

At last they let her leave them, with kisses and singing and fond farewells. As she stumbled along the steep cobbled streets Hannah hummed a tune to herself. Such good friends she had, she thought again, and her kind-hearted mother was sure to be waiting up for her at home. Life was good.

Hannah stopped her humming with a start. What was that scraping she heard on the cobbles behind her? It sounded like an animal slipping and sliding on wet stone. There was always sewage and muck from horses and people running down these narrow streets, and stray cats and dogs roamed at night, foxes and rats too. Hannah turned round, but she was not really afraid. She was too happy, too fuzzy from the gin to be afraid.

"Here, puss ..." she called, and she waited for a scraggy cat to emerge from the shadows. But nothing came. After a moment, Hannah walked on.

There it was again, that same scraping, slipping sound. Behind her, closer this time. Hannah turned once more. Her nerves were tense, and she was a little nervous now. She peered into the darkness. Something was there. She could make out the shape of it. Bigger than a cat, almost invisible in the dark, but her keen eyes could see it. Her heart beat faster but she was not afraid. It was just a man, or a boy ... yes a boy, making his way home, as she was. But still her steps grew faster.

The sound behind her grew faster in time with her steps. This time Hannah didn't stop, or turn. She just wanted home now, as fast as possible.

But the faster she moved, the faster the steps behind her closed in on her, too close for comfort.

Was this boy trying to scare her? Well, she wasn't having that. Hannah decided to be bold.

She stopped dead in her tracks and swung round.

"Who are you!" It was a demand, not a question. "I have no money," she added in case the boy was a thief. Any thief should know that no one had money in this part of Edinburgh, at this time of night. Yet Hannah prayed, almost hoped that he was a thief, and not something worse. She turned from him again and rushed on, picking up her pace until she was nearly running.

In her haste and rising fear, she slid on the cobbles and had to grab the alley wall to stop herself from falling. She looked behind her to see how far behind he was, and that was when she knew that the Beast was back.

The shape was a little clearer, bent over, but still hidden in the dark shadows of a close. Just as all the rumours and whispers had said, it was not quite human. It was small, ugly, deformed. She could hear its breathing, the rasping breath of a wild animal.

Hannah was running in the same moment she saw it, and as she ran she screamed. Her screams rang down the narrow closes and alleys. The people of the Old Town lit candles, opened windows and flung doors wide. Hannah ran on and in her panic she lost track of where she was going. As she fled she found herself lost in the tangle of streets she knew so well. Still the Beast ran faster behind her. Soon it would be on her.

"Help me!" Hannah screamed as a woman came out of her house. She opened her arms wide and Hannah fell into them.

"He's there!" She pointed into the darkness behind her. "I saw him. He was upon me."

Now a man stepped from the house with a lantern in his hands and he ran out into the night.

"Come on, we'll get him this time," he shouted out to his neighbours.

Other men rushed to follow him and the chase was on. As they ran, more men tumbled out of houses, out of taverns. They held lanterns over their heads and clutched sticks, ready to catch the Beast.

"There he is!" a voice shouted, and they saw a hunched creature run into the darkness. The creature was fast, but the men would not give up. The cry spread through the Old Town. The streets came alive with people. The night was filled with their determination not to lose him this time.

They chased their prey to one of the oldest and narrowest of the closes. A sharp yell of pain came out of the darkness with the sound of something crashing to the ground.

"He's fallen!" someone shouted. "We've got him now."

The crowd pressed into the close and surrounded the creature. He lay in a heap on the steep stone stairs, trying to coil himself up like a child in his mother's womb. Long hair hid his face.

One of the men stepped forward and hauled the creature to his feet.

"Look at its nails." There was a gasp. "They're claws."

"The claws of a Beast."

His legs were bent and crooked and he could not stand straight. His head hung low. He spoke no words, only grunted like an animal.

The crowd of men half dragged, half carried him back along the streets.

"We've got him!" they cried in triumph, as they waved their lanterns and sticks.

There were cheers from every window, from every door. There were cries of disgust and horror as the townspeople watched this strange creature being hauled like the carcass of a dead animal across the filthy cobbles.

At last, the crowd threw him on the ground in front of Hannah. "Is this the Beast you saw?" they demanded.

The hubbub had reached Hannah's mother and she had rushed across the Old Town, desperate to help her daughter. Hannah was now wrapped in her arms. She peered out of half-shut eyes, too overcome with terror to look.

The creature lay curled up on the stones of the cobbles. She could see that his form was misshapen, his hair long and ragged over his face. It had been so dark, could she be sure?

Then she saw the nails on his hands, long and curved and, worse, the same nails on his feet, and she remembered the scraping sounds she had heard – just as if those nails were scratching on the cobbles as he ran behind her. Not a human sound at all. More like the sound of the claws of an animal.

"That's him." There was not a scrap of doubt in Hannah's voice. "Aye, that's him."

- 5 -

Child of Hell

"And so, they have caught the Beast at last."

Mary finishes, for of course it is she who has brought the fiendish story to our house in the New Town. She has run all the way to tell everyone about the chase in the Old Town the night before.

"And my father was one of the men who caught him," she adds with a thrill of pride.

"I thought this creature had gone," Mrs Kerr says, her voice flat.

"We all thought that, ma'am, but he came back. But it is better that we caught him." Mary speaks as if she too had been one of the hunters. "If he's in the jail then we will all be safe. Better to have him behind bars where we can watch him, than have him running loose."

. It is clear that Mary is repeating what her mother or father has said, but she speaks with such a grown-up air that Mrs Kerr has to smile.

"You do lead an exciting life, Mary," she says.

"Aye, I'm very lucky," Mary agrees.

☽

My nightmares come back that night. The usual nightmares. I'm running in the dark. One minute I am the hunter and the next, I am the hunted. I wake in a cold sweat. But this morning, my cries have not woken my mother or my father, and I am glad of that. For now I do not have to tell them I had another dream.

But Mother notices how pale and tired I am at breakfast. "Are you well? Did you sleep?" She feels my brow. "Have you a fever?"

"I slept well, Mother."

"I knew the sleeping tonic would help you," my father says.

"Indeed it has, Father."

I hate to lie to my father, but I cannot live my life taking medicine to help me sleep. I didn't take the tonic last night. But the thought will not leave me – if I had taken it, might there have been no nightmares?

"I'm happy to hear this," my father says. Then he turns to my mother, "Well, I can tell you now that this creature was seen again last night."

My mother gasps and her hand clutches her throat in a dramatic manner.

"Shh, my dear," my father says, and he calms her with a hand on her arm. "Have no fear. The creature is now safe in the hands of the law."

"Safe?" The story excites me too. "And what kind of creature is he?" I ask.

My father smiles. "If you listen to Mary, he is ten feet tall, with the teeth and fiery breath of a dragon and claws like a lion. Her father seems to have had a hand in catching him."

"And is he?" I ask. "Ten feet tall?"

"Not at all." My father shakes his head. "I will see him for myself today. The sheriff has asked me to come in and examine him."

This sends my mother into another shriek. "Oh, my dear, be careful. He is a monster."

"I will be surrounded by police officers," Father assures her. "I will be perfectly safe."

"But is he ... human?" I demand. "They all say he is not."

Why am I so keen to know?

"I'm sure he is, Harry," my father says. "There will be a logical answer to this mystery. There always is."

$$)$$

It was all the talk below stairs in the servants' quarters, I know that. But when I appeared, their mouths shut like clam shells. They would lower their eyes and move on. I am so eager to hear more of the story and Mary is my only hope. She cannot stop herself from telling me. I find her in the drawing room sweeping out the ashes from the grate and preparing to light the afternoon fire. She gets to her feet as soon as I enter.

"Good morning, sir." She bobs her head.

"Good morning, Mary." It is a moment before I dare to go on. "I believe you had a very exciting night last night."

Her face flushes. Even her freckles seem to glow. "Oh, sir, what a night it was indeed." Then she stops. Her hand flies to her mouth. "Get back in there, words," she cries. "Don't you dare come out!"

I smile. Mary always makes me smile. "No Mary," I say. "Please tell me everything. No one else will. It will be our secret. Did you see the creature? Is he really a monster?"

She says nothing for a moment. I can see she is unsure whether to obey me, or to obey everyone else in the house, Mrs Kerr and her mistress, my mother.

At last, I win. Mary answers my question.

"I didn't see him myself, no, sir," she says. "My mother wouldn't allow her bairns to look at him in case their eyes crossed for ever." When she sees my smile she shakes her head. "That can happen you know, sir."

I nod and try to look serious. "I believe so."

"But my father saw him clear as day," she goes on. "He said he was bent double, out of shape, a strange creature with hair over his face and long nails like the claws of a bird on his feet and on his hands. And blood and scratches all over him." She pauses. "That would be from all the killing he does."

I can picture him myself, crawling through the alleys of the Old Town, scratching with those long nails at windows and doors. My heart beats faster.

"But has he killed anyone, Mary?"

Mary does not hesitate for a second. "Oh yes, sir, for sure. Cats and stray dogs he has killed, we know that. But there will be more, everyone is saying it." She nods her head. "Oh yes, sir. The bodies will turn up soon. You wait and see."

"Has he confessed?" I ask her.

Now she shakes her head. "Not yet, sir." She sounds disappointed. "He doesn't talk at all. He grunts and roars like an animal. Oh I am so glad he's been caught, sir."

"So am I," I tell her. "You will tell me if you hear anything else, Mary?"

"Oh, I don't know, sir." Her nose scrunches. "I'm always being told I talk too much."

"I won't tell, I promise," I say. I take a step closer to her. "You are the only one I can rely on, Mary."

Her face beams with pleasure. "Then you can rely on me, sir. If I hear any more about the Beast, I will be sure to let you know."

But I hear more about the creature before Mary does.

- 6 -

My Father Meets the Monster

I can hardly wait for my father to come home. I watch for his carriage from the window. A fog has come down and a lacy evening mist drifts over the gas lights in the street below. Every time I hear the sound of wheels on cobbles in our street, I hope it is him. Tonight, of all nights, he is late. My mother wishes he were back too. I can sense her pacing her room, back and forth. Her mind will be running in wild loops, until she is sure he has been attacked by the creature. She will expect to see him stumble round the corner towards our house, his clothes in filthy tatters, his face cut and bleeding. I smile at the wildness of my own imagination.

And there he is at last, climbing out of his carriage, swinging his cane. Safe, and looking every inch the gentleman. I am there beside my mother when he comes in the front door.

My father smiles. "This is a fine welcome."

"I was so worried," my mother says as she clutches at his arm. "When I was in town today all the talk was of the creature, and the horror that happened in the Old Town last night. Oh, the monstrous things he has done." My mother shudders. She is nothing if not dramatic. "And the way he looks, they say he is a creature out of a nightmare."

My father keeps us in suspense for a moment longer. He pulls off his cloak and slips his cane into the umbrella stand by the door. "I cannot say anything about the things he's done, but I can tell you he is no monster."

"No monster!" My mother and I say it as one.

"Indeed he is not," my father tells us. "He is a poor soul. A poor, dirty, malformed boy. One of those children who have no one to care for them, and must live by whatever means they can. They sleep on the streets, in the sewers, and eat what they can find or steal. He has never eaten a decent meal. Perhaps this is why he is so malformed. He has had no proper food. His legs are bent. He is filthy, or he was – they have washed him now, and they have cut his hair. It was growing down his back, no wonder he looked like a wild animal. The nails on his hands and on his feet had never been cut so they grew long and curved."

"Like claws," I say.

"Yes, like claws, but they will be cut too. And the poor fellow can hardly stand straight either."

"He is a hunchback?" I ask. I have seen many hunchback beggars in this city.

My father shakes his head. "No. If he has lived all his life in the tunnels and vaults under the streets of this city, then he has never been able to stand tall. When his nails and hair are cut and he is washed all this will make a difference to how he appears. He will look human again. He will look like what he is – a boy." We follow my father into the drawing room, not wishing to miss a word. "In truth," he says, "he is a poor pathetic creature who has no words to express himself."

This child hardly sounds like a monster.

"You mean he is just a boy? A poor boy?" I ask. "Then he cannot possibly be this Beast that's been haunting us."

"My boy, of course he is the creature they've been hunting," my mother says. "Now he has been caught and now he is safe in jail and we are safe too." She will not allow for the law to make any mistakes. "He has to be the Beast."

"But if he is only a boy, Mother –"

"A boy can be guilty of terrible crimes too," she insists.

"It would seem he is guilty, Harry," my father agrees. "The girl who was running from him has sworn he is the creature who chased her. And everyone says she is a good, decent girl who would not lie."

"And what does the boy say, Father?"

"It is hard to understand him when he speaks, but when he does, he says a monster knocked him over in the dark. It clawed at him and that is why, when the crowd found him a moment later, he was covered in fresh blood and scratches."

"Lies!" my mother snaps. "All lies, and he's not such a pathetic boy if he can make up lies like that."

"Enough," my father says. "I have been hard at work all day and now I am hungry. Let us eat and thank God for the good life we have. That boy today, a boy who has never had a father or mother to care for him, made me realise that so many children are not so fortunate as our own Harry."

My father's voice is nearly breaking with emotion. He sees so much of the poor and neglected of our beautiful city – and I feel how much this boy has affected him, so I ask no more.

))

Another night and no nightmares.

I awake feeling well and after breakfast I go in search of Mary. She deserves to know what I have learned from my father about the Beast. She is scrubbing the stone steps, a task that must be done every day. She stops when she hears me coming. She looks up and pushes a lock of hair away from her eyes.

"I told you that I would share any news with you, Mary." My voice drops to a whisper. "My father saw him yesterday."

Her pretty mouth opens wide in shock. "And he has lived to tell the tale?"

I cannot help but smile. "Indeed he has."

"And what does this monster look like, sir?"

"My father says ... that he is not a monster at all. He is a boy – dirty, bent, hungry – but just a boy."

Mary puts the scrubbing brush down and sits back. "That's right, sir. They're all saying the same thing. He's one of the ferals."

"The ferals?" I ask, wondering what she means.

"They are boys, girls too," Mary says in almost a whisper. "Children who live under the city in the tunnels, the sewers and old vaults. They crawl into the darkness and filth under the streets of the Old Town and only come out at night to steal food."

"Mary," I say. "I cannot believe there are children who live like that here in Edinburgh."

She lifts an eyebrow and looks at me as if she is amazed I did not know about these 'ferals' before. I feel like a little boy told off by his mother.

"Children have to live how they can if they are abandoned," she says. "Not everyone is as lucky as you and me, sir."

I blush at this. Mary works so hard, both at my house and her own, and she considers herself as fortunate as I am. She is indeed a fine girl. My father is right, as always. We are blessed to have such a good life.

"Do you really think he can be guilty, Mary?" I ask. "He doesn't seem like a monster."

"He must be, sir. Everyone says Hannah would not lie." But her bonnie face is sad and she sounds as sorry as I am that it is true.

"I wonder what they will do to him, Mary."

"He'll swing for sure, sir," she tells me. She lifts her eyes again and seems almost cheery at the prospect of a hanging.

Just then the front door swings open and Mrs Kerr looms over us. "Mary Cole, what is this you're saying?"

"It's my fault, Mrs Kerr," I say. "I spoke to Mary first. We were wondering if this wild boy will be hanged."

"He'll swing for sure," Mary says again.

"Of course he won't," Mrs Kerr says with a glare at both of us. "We don't hang children in this country ... not any more. He'll likely be transported to Australia on one of those terrible ships. And a good thing too. Get him as far away from Edinburgh as possible."

- 7 -

Another Attack

I awake after another night free of dreams. My first thought is of that poor boy – why do I think of him so much? – but I soon dismiss him from my mind. He is not my business, and perhaps a prison ship to Australia is better than a life in the dark, under the city, never able to stand tall. I shiver again at the thought of it.

It is a bright day, warm for the time of year, and a big yellow sun peeps out from behind the clouds. I go out into the garden to read and am sitting on my father's bench under the apple trees when I hear something.

"Hss. *Hss.*"

I look around, and there is Mary, crouching between the bushes like a thief.

"Excuse me, sir." Her eyes dart to the house to make sure Mrs Kerr is nowhere about. "There was another attack last night –"

My heart thuds. "Another attack?" I interrupt her. "Who was attacked? What happened?" I do not even wait for her answer. "And the boy is still in jail? You know what this means, Mary?"

She nods. "That boy – the feral boy – he cannot be the Beast, sir."

"No, he cannot."

"They won't transport him now, sir, will they?"

"No. They will have to set him free."

Her face lights up with a smile. "I never wanted him to be guilty, sir."

"Neither did I, Mary," I tell her, but I cannot return her smile.

☽

I have to wait till dinner to speak to my father. But he says nothing about it – and I am surprised. It must be all the talk of the city. It is only after we finish the fine apple pie Mrs Kerr has made for our pudding that I dare to ask.

"I heard a rumour that there was another attack last night," I say. My voice is light as if it were nothing.

"Oh no," my mother says. "I thought it was all over."

My father looks up from his plate, but he stays silent.

"Did they release the boy?" I ask.

With this I have his full interest. "Release him?" he says. "Why would they do that?"

"The boy was behind bars in prison last night. So he couldn't have carried out the attack. He must be innocent."

But my father dismisses me with a wave of his hand. "Last night wasn't a real attack. The police believe it was other street children. Perhaps the boy's friends wanted to save him, to prove his innocence. They were running along the streets, howling like wolves, jumping out to scare people. Clever, but useless." My father looks at me. "One of them was caught by an officer and confessed the trick almost at once."

"So you still think that he is guilty?" I ask.

"It does not matter what I think, Harry," my father says. "An eye-witness named him, and he was caught almost red handed." He looked at me in thought. "Why are you so interested, Harry? Why do you so much want this boy to be innocent?"

I return my father's gaze, but I cannot answer because I do not know. All I know is that my life is so good, my parents love me, and I have so much to be grateful for. And that poor pathetic wretch of a child has never known a parent's love, never eaten as I have eaten, or slept in the warm comfort of a soft bed as I have.

My heart bleeds for him.

If he is innocent.

- 8 -

Important News

Soon I put the boy from my mind. Other things are happening in my life. My father comes home one Friday afternoon with a letter in his hand.

"It has come. It has come," he says. I have never heard him sound so excited.

My mother comes flying down the stairs in a most undignified manner. And my mother is never undignified. She is as excited as my father.

"It has come at last?" she calls out.

"What has come?" I ask.

My father beckons me into the drawing room. As soon as Mother and I are there, he closes the door. His face is beaming with pleasure.

"Let me explain, Harry. Your mother knows of course, but I wanted to keep it from you. There was no point in all of us being disappointed."

"Disappointed about what?" I say. "Please, Father, do not keep me in suspense any longer."

My father stands with his back to the fireplace. "A few weeks ago I applied for a post in London. A very fine post in one of the best hospitals. Many other doctors applied. But I ..." He waves the letter again. "I was successful."

"Hurrah!" My mother leaps from her seat and throws her arms around his neck. "We are moving to London."

My father takes her in his arms and they begin to dance round the drawing room. I am shocked. I have never seen my parents behaving in such a manner, and for what? For a move to London?

My father notices how still I am. "Are you not excited, Harry?" he asks.

"We are leaving Edinburgh?"

"Yes." He dances across the room towards me. "I thought you would be happy."

"But I like Edinburgh."

"You will love London," he says, and he flings his arms wide. "It has just as much history as Edinburgh and that history is just as dark. You will visit the Tower of London. The horrors that have happened there will shock you."

My father knows that I love strange and grisly things. He thinks this will tempt me, will make me want to go. He is wrong.

But I see how happy he is. My mother too. How can I tell them that I do not just *like* Edinburgh? I love it. I love everything about it. I love the Old Town, with its narrow dark closes and wynds, I love the New Town with its fine open streets and houses. I do not want to leave here. Yet I will have to. I will have no choice.

My mother stops and claps her hands. "I have a wonderful idea," she declares. "We shall have a party. A ball for all our friends before we go."

My father smiles and embraces her. "Indeed we shall, my dear wife."

☽

The days fly past. Too fast. Trunks are packed, and the house is a hive of activity. Mrs Kerr bursts into tears whenever she sees me.

"I'm going to miss you, young Master Harry. We all are," she says, and she wipes her face on the corner of her apron.

And I am going to miss them.

Only Mary seems excited at the prospect of our move.

"I would love to go to London," she tells me one day when I find her cleaning out the fireplace. "It is my dream. How can you not be happy about going there?"

"You go in my place then," I tell her. "I have no wish to go."

This makes her laugh. And I think what a sweet laugh she has, like the water from a stream tumbling clear over rocks.

"I could dress up as the young master." She laughs. "No one would know the difference at all." She giggles again and presses her hands into her skirt as if to make a pair of breeches. "No, sir, don't look so shocked. I could never pass for anything but a serving girl."

I look at Mary, my gaze level. I do not believe that. I think everyone has it in them to change, to be someone different. I think of the boy with no home but the city's dank tunnels, no parents to guide him. If we had changed places at birth, he would now be tall like me. He would have had a fine education and the love of two parents. And me? I would be like him, unloved, unwanted and uncared for.

Mary is still chattering on. "And what would you do if you stayed here, sir?"

I smile. "I would set that boy free," I say. "He cannot be guilty, Mary."

"What makes you so certain of that, sir?"

I have no answer to her question other than some feeling deep within me I cannot explain. "He is not the Beast, I am sure of it," I tell her.

"There have been no more attacks, sir, apart from the one his friends staged. The streets have been safe. Perhaps you are wrong."

I shrug and press my fist to my chest. "I feel it in here, Mary. The boy is innocent."

"I think it's just that you have a very big heart, sir." She smiles and empties ash into a bucket. "But there is no point in dwelling on such things now."

She is right. I have no power to save the boy. I must go to London no matter how much I would rather stay.

"It is a fine day, Mary," I say. "I'm going for a walk. If anyone asks …" I nod towards the bustle in the other rooms. "I have to get out of this house for a while. All my mother talks about is this ball."

"You're not looking forward to it, sir?" she asks.

"No, I am not," I say. "I'm not looking forward to going to London, or the ball. What a way to spend an evening. Dressing up and dancing." I make a face. "Sounds awful."

Mary's voice becomes a whisper. "I am to come to the ball too, sir."

"You are?"

"Not as a grand lady." She giggles again at the thought of that. "No, sir, to help. I will have a new white apron and bonnet. This is your first ball too, sir. You must try to be excited."

Mary is right – I should be excited.

But I am not.

- 9 -

The Night of the Ball

The day of the ball arrives and from the first light of morning I can sense the energy in the house. The servants polish silver and light candles. Bowls of fresh flowers on every table send their sweet scent into every corner. My father has hired a small orchestra to play and they spend the afternoon tuning up and rehearsing. The floor of the drawing room has been cleared for dancing – servants have rolled up the rugs and carried them to one of the store rooms.

When night falls, a sliver of moon hangs in a midnight blue sky. The stars sparkle. Perfect weather, apart from the cold Edinburgh east wind. I have never seen my mother so happy, or so beautiful. She floats down our wide staircase in her dress of green silk. It moves around her in waves, and her dark hair is held up with green ribbons to match her dress. I can see that my father is proud of her as she stands with him to greet their guests.

I would much prefer to stay in my room, but my father insists that I stand beside them and greet his friends and colleagues. I can leave the ball early, he promises me, and that is enough for me.

And so they come, the great and the good of Edinburgh, in their grand carriages and their fine clothes. The men wear top hats and cloaks, and some are in army uniform. The ladies are in dresses of all colours and shades, golds and reds and blues and lilacs. The servants come forward with glasses of champagne on trays and even they look wonderful in new dresses and suits. Mrs Kerr glows in the whitest of white as she peeks from behind a curtain to see the fine ladies and gentlemen.

There is Mary, as shiny as a polished pin. Her hair is tied up inside a crisp white cap, and her new apron is tied around her. She is helping to take umbrellas and canes from guests as they enter, and she looks very serious and grown up. I long to run over and make her laugh, to hear her tumbling giggles.

I watch all this for a long time from my place beside my parents, and all the while I nod and shake hands as the guests arrive.

"How tall you have grown, Harry," one guest says.

"What a fine son you have," says another.

These remarks can't help but make me feel proud. I am glad I have come, but glad still to be leaving early.

The orchestra strikes up a tune and couples take to the floor to dance, but I have no wish to join them. Even when I am a man, I think I will not care to dance.

My father hands me a glass of champagne. He stands with me as I take a sip. I groan and shudder and my head shakes. I push the glass back at him.

"I do not care for that at all, sir," I say, and my father laughs and slaps me on the back.

It seems neither drink nor dance are for me.

At last, they allow me to return to my room. As I lie in bed I can hear the sounds of the ball as they drift up from the rooms below.

An opera singer's voice fills the house with sweetness. A great cheer greets the end of her songs and the orchestra strikes up again. I hear the merry laughter and I know my mother and father are having a wonderful evening with their guests. Next, a man with a rich tenor voice sings an old Scots ballad of love and loss. The song makes me ache with sadness. I will hate to leave this city. Yet leave it I must.

At last, I feel my eyes close as the singing lulls me to sleep.

☽

I dream. I am running again. I can hear a hound barking behind me, and it's too close. Men are shouting. The fog has come down and I do not know where I am, or where I am going. My heart beats with terror.

The hound comes closer, and the voices urge him on.

"He has the scent of him," a man calls out. "Get him, Rolf. Don't lose him."

I keep running. I am sure I have come this way before. I recognise the sign hanging outside a butcher's shop. I slip on the cobbles, and skin my knees. The hunters are closing in. I must run faster. But I feel that I am going round in circles. Then I hear the men shout and it is clear they have set their hound free. It is off the lead.

"Run, Rolf, run," they shout. "Get him, boy."

I can hear the pounding of huge paws as the dog races towards me. I turn one more corner and I find I can go no further. A high wall bars my way. There is nowhere for me to run. As I turn, the nightmare pounding is only seconds away. This hound, this nightmare hound, will be upon me any moment. One more second and we will be face to face.

$$\text{☽}$$

I wake covered in cold sweat and aching with fear. Early dawn light is in the sky as I slip from my bed. I cross to my dresser to splash cold water on my face. My heart is beating so fast it feels it will burst out of my chest at any moment. I take a deep breath, look in the mirror above my basin, and what I see there chills me.

I am covered in blood.

But whose blood?

- 10 -

Whose Blood?

"Harry, are you well?" It is my mother calling to me, knocking in panic on my locked door. "Let me in."

I have washed the blood away, but I cannot let her see me. There are still scratches and cuts on my arms, on my knees, on my body. What has happened? What have I done?

I need time to think.

"My head hurts," I call out. "I want to sleep."

"It is the champagne," my mother calls. "Your father should never have let you taste it."

I wish I could blame that sip of champagne.

At last my mother leaves me in peace and I try to sleep, yet I am afraid. What dreams would leave me like this? With blood on my face, scratches on my limbs and bruises on my body?

And whose blood is it?

It is after noon before I come out of my room. I have washed and cleaned myself up as best I can. I use the back stairs that lead down to the kitchen to avoid my mother. I cannot face her. I am thirsty, so thirsty, and hungry too. Mrs Kerr will feed me, and she will not ask too many questions.

As I approach the kitchen, I hear voices, and one of them is Mary's. She is doing most of the talking. That thought makes me smile for the first time that day. Her chatter makes everything seem so normal, and I need things to be normal because I do not understand what is happening to me.

I stand behind the door, press myself against the wall so I cannot be seen, and I listen.

"And someone saw him," Mary says, and her voice is high and excited. "The cry went up. 'He's here!' The men all took up arms to go after him. My father too." I can hear the pride in Mary's voice at this. "And one of our neighbours, Big George we call him. He's a lion of a man, and he says, 'We'll not lose him. My Rolf will smell him out.' Rolf is his dog, and he's like a lion too, the most brutal beast of a dog you have ever seen. No one likes it. It's been known to bite children, and it almost took the arm off one of –"

Mrs Kerr breaks in. "Yes, yes, Mary. We understand. It's a big dog. Now go on with your story."

I imagine the cook rolling her eyes and Mary pouting. But, after only a moment, she goes on.

"So Big George keeps this dog on a lead," she says, "and they lead the crowd after him, along the wynds and closes. People are at their windows shouting them on. And then, the dog strains at the lead. He has the scent of him. And that means he's near. 'I can't hold him,' Big George shouts. 'Let him go,' they call to him. 'Let the dog get him.' And, sure enough, that monster of a dog is soon off the lead, and it's off, barking and howling as it races into the fog."

I am holding my breath as I listen. I can picture it all. Mary, as always, brings her story alive.

"Don't keep us hanging," Mrs Kerr says. She too is desperate to hear the end of Mary's tale, for all she would never admit it.

But Mary knows how to draw her tale out. She pauses before she goes on.

"The crowd are close behind. Big George shouts, 'Rolf will not lose him,' and a cheer goes up. Then they hear wild barking and they know the dog has cornered him. 'Come on!' Big George shouts. 'He's got him.'

"And then there was a howl such as no one had ever heard before. It stops the crowd in its tracks. It is a howl of fear and of pain. 'It's the Beast,' someone whispers. 'It must be the Beast.'

"And another whispers, 'Aye, but what Beast?'

"They turn a corner into a narrow gloomy close, and there on the cobbles lies Rolf. He's whimpering, covered in blood, his throat ripped out ... a second later the life drains from him onto the cobbles. He is dead."

For a moment there is silence in the kitchen. Then Mrs Kerr tuts. "Och, Mary, I don't believe a word of that. You tell a tall story, my girl!"

"It's the truth as sure as I am standing here, Mrs Kerr." Mary sounds offended. "Ask anybody in the Old Town. It was the Beast that did for that poor dog. It's not human ... it's the Bogeyman."

My head spins and my breath comes in gasps. I hit the door in a half-faint, and the sound brings Mrs Kerr out of the kitchen with Mary close behind her.

"Have you been listening, sir?" Mrs Kerr asks. She doesn't wait for my answer before she turns to Mary. "You and your fine bogey tales. Now look what you have done."

I try to protest. I try to tell her not to blame Mary, but the words will not come.

Mrs Kerr puts her hands on my brow. "Oh you are burning up, sir." I feel her eyes on my cuts. "And you have been scratching at your face. Let me clean them up, sir."

She turns to one of the kitchen boys, who has also been listening to Mary's tale. "Here, Robbie, come and help me get him back to his room."

At last I manage a few words. "Please don't tell my mother," I beg. "I do not want to alarm her."

This brings a warm smile to Mrs Kerr's face. "You are a good boy, Harry," she says. "As you wish. I will not tell your mother."

Soon, I am settled back in my bed. I know Mrs Kerr will be true to her word and say nothing to my mother, but all afternoon and into evening I am in fitful, restless sleep. Mary told her story with such power, I can see it all in my mind. But there is one thought I do not understand. One thing that terrifies me more than any other.

In Mary's story, the dog that attacked the Beast was called Rolf. And in my nightmare, too, the dog was called Rolf. How can that be? How could I know such a thing? My father always says there is a logical explanation for everything. But what is the logical explanation for this?

))

My mother comes to my room in the evening. She is all worry and concern. She thinks I have a fever and she insists my father calls for another doctor to examine me. She says we need a second opinion, no matter how I protest that we do not. They fuss and fret over me. It seems too long before I am alone again. The red velvet curtains at my window are pulled wide to let in the last of the light. Long shadows move along the floor. I am afraid to be alone when night falls.

But am I alone? A terrible idea has begun to form in my head. Something that could be the explanation for this. There is no logic, it is too strange to believe, yet it answers all my questions.

Is there another 'me' inside me? A 'me' who comes to life in my nightmares? Mary's story has told me a truth I dared not face, yet I always suspected. These are not nightmares I have been having. These are memories.

I was the one running through the night.

I was the one in terror as I was chased by the hound.

I am the one who killed Rolf.

I am the Beast.

- 11 -

Truly Two

How could this be?

Even as I ask myself, I know the answer.

I have always known.

I am not truly one, but truly two.

There has always been another one inside me.

From my very first days I knew I had evil
within me. I could feel it. The urge to hurt,
and to kill. Yes, even to kill. I shudder at the
thought of what I have done. But I come from a
good, caring family. My father is a doctor of high
standing, and my mother a good woman who does

charitable works. It would hurt them beyond anything if my secret evil were ever discovered. So all my young life I have been compelled to find ways to hide – even from myself – that side of my nature, the evil side that drove me to these terrible acts.

Hide.

A good name for the horror that lives within me.

As a child I was not naughty. I obeyed every rule, but set against that I could feel a struggle burn inside me, a longing to be free. I would, like any other boy, get up to mischief, but I was never hurtful or cruel. But there were times when the other one would escape from the hidden places inside, and I found I had no power to hold him back. He had no shame or guilt for the terrible things he did.

No one could believe I might be the one who had done those things – not until the day they caught me. The memory of that day has been locked away for so long, but now it comes back to me as clear as if it were yesterday.

I was seven or so, and I was in the garden. I found a nest of baby birds and I smashed my foot down again and again into it. I killed them all, and it was as if the horror of my act woke me up, bringing me back to myself. The other, evil one shrivelled deep within me and left me to face the guilt and the blame.

I was thinking ... *How did I get here? Why am I doing such a murderous thing?*

But I had no time to answer my own questions. A neighbour had seen what I had done. He lifted me by the collar and dragged me to my father.

"Your son has the evil eye," he told him, and he threw me to the ground. "I have seen it before and now I have the proof."

My father lifted me up and told the man never to lay hands on me again. But the moment we were alone he shook his head in sorrow, and I saw pain in his eyes.

My mother refused to believe her gentle son had been responsible for anything so awful, so cruel. "A young boy's prank gone wrong," she insisted.

But my father scolded me with harsh words, and warned me that such a thing must never happen again. My cruelty shamed and horrified him, and I was not worthy of the family name. "I do not understand how you – my son – could act in such a brutal manner," he told me.

I could not understand it myself either. And I hated myself, or that evil part of myself I could not control. I could not bear it that I had shamed my parents. I could not bear it that I had disappointed them. I made a promise to my father that day, and to my mother, that this would never happen again.

And for a long time I kept that promise. I was only a child, but still I fought against this other one, and I learned to keep the evil in my nature hidden deep within. Yet, I missed him. I know I did. After I had buried that dark half of me, I felt like only half a person.

If only, I have often thought, I could separate these two selves into different bodies. Then my life would be free of all this guilt I feel. The evil part of me could do all he pleases and he would not be restrained by his more moral twin. If only that were possible – but how? All I can think is that perhaps one day the experiments of science will find a way to do this.

But, for now, I am tied to him. We are the two halves of a whole. Without him I am small and weak. With him I am fearless and bold – and, yes, evil.

With him, I am whole. I am one.

Is this the answer? Is this why all this has happened? Had I kept him hidden for too long?

Had it come to the point where he had to break free? He was now free, but this time he had turned the tables on me. On the nights he roamed free, I was the one who was pushed deep within *him*. I was the one who was hidden. He escaped while I was at my weakest, when I was asleep. He leaped from my window to the damp cobbles below, and ran along the streets to the darkness of the Old Town. Fearless, while I live in fear. Home again before dawn, while I am none the wiser.

But I know now. And the knowledge fills me with fear. I remember everything. I remember the joy I felt when I saw terror in people's eyes as they caught sight of me. I bent my body like an ape and snarled and growled like a wild animal to frighten them even more. Cats arched their backs at me. Dogs whimpered, turned and ran from me. Yes, there is something in that other me that finds joy in creating terror in others.

But if he can escape without my knowledge, then there must be a way for me to keep him under control. My father's sleeping tonic helped. But I cannot live my life taking powders to send me to sleep each night. Perhaps one day I will find a drug that will only let him loose when I choose. But until such a time I have to stop him.

I vow that this cannot go on. This cannot be. I must find a way to bury him again, like a corpse, dead within me. And this time he must stay dead, he must remain dead and cold, because one day this evil part of me will destroy me if I do not destroy it first.

He must die, if I am to live.

- 12 -

Deep Within Me

For two nights I do not sleep.

I keep the door to my balcony open so the cold night air will keep me awake. I sit up in my chair, then I pace back and forth across the room, back and forth. I will not sleep. *I will not sleep.* Still I can feel him pressing against me as he tries to force himself out, desperate to escape. And the more tired I become the stronger he grows. I do not leave the room, I seldom see my parents and my mother grows more and more worried.

"The sooner we leave for London the better," she says and I almost cry out with joy. Here, I see, is an answer.

"Yes, yes, if I go I can leave him behind," I tell myself. I long to leave him here in Edinburgh, in my past.

Tonight, my father has insisted that I come down for dinner. He will not let me stay alone in my room any longer.

"You must eat, Harry," he says.

As I sit at the table I imagine I see spirits walking around the room. Misty spirits that rise into the air and disappear like smoke.

I see my mother standing at the door, smiling at me. But how can that be when she is also sitting across from me at the table with that same loving smile?

My father's words seem to come from a distant place – like the far-off echo of a voice. I cannot make out what he is saying. He sits at the head of the table and sips his soup, dabs his lips with his napkin. I gasp when he appears behind himself and strides across the room, while more ghosts and spirits join him. This other father stops and places his hands on the back of his own chair, and he smiles at me. That same fond smile, but in the blink of an eye that smile changes. There is no fondness in it now. It is sinister. His eyes sink deep into his face, and become like black holes. His mouth is stretched back so all I can see are his teeth. His face is that of a skull. My father has become a monster.

"You are so pale, Harry," my mother says, but which mother – the one standing at the door, or the one sitting across from me? Which one is real? And why should this surprise me so much? If there are two of me, why should there not be two of her?

"I see ghosts, Mother," I tell her, and I wave my hand to take in the room. "I see strange ghosts all around me."

She lets out a low moan and her eyes well up with tears. My father gets up from his seat to comfort her.

"It's lack of sleep, my dear, that is all," he says. "These ghosts are in his mind. Harry needs to sleep. I shall make up a tonic for him again."

"No. No," I start to say, and then I remember that with the tonic I slept, and the other slept too, deep within me. "Yes, Father," I say. "The tonic. I think that would help me."

My mother smiles again. "Harry will be fine when we get to London," she says. It has become her answer to everything.

My father shakes his head. "That may not be for a while yet. I do not wish to leave until I see what fate has in store for that poor boy in prison."

"But has he not been let go?" I say.

How could I have forgotten about the boy?

"The Beast has been seen again," I say. "He killed a hound with his bare hands. There were many witnesses." I shudder now at the memory. The feel of that huge animal struggling for life beneath me, the dark taste of its blood.

"You've been listening to Mary," my father almost snaps. "No, the police think another dog was responsible for that attack, and so they still think the boy is guilty. And the witnesses were drunken ruffians from the Old Town. No, the boy will be deported to Australia for sure."

"But he is not guilty!" I cry out.

"How can you be so certain, Harry?" my father asks, and his voice is sharp.

I have no answer to that. I can only say, "He seems to have had such a sad life. I feel he needs help, not punishment."

Yet a life of punishment is what he will get, because of me. I stand up from the dinner table, and I go back to my room.

I lock the door and pace back and forth, back and forth, thinking. How can I help the boy?

Then it comes to me. The only answer that I can find. But it's a daring, dangerous plan, and I don't know if I am strong enough to carry it out.

I have to let him out one more time. *The other one. The evil one.* Only, this time, I have to be with him, awake, in control. I have to be the Master.

I have to let him be seen, by many witnesses. This is the only way I can prove to the world that the boy is innocent.

- 13 -

A Horror of the Spirit

My father comes to my room with the sleeping tonic just before the clock strikes nine.

"Now, drink it up, my boy, and tonight you will have the best sleep of your life." He is so kind to me, such a good papa. I can't help but think that he deserves a better son than me.

"Thank you, Father," I say. "You're too good to me."

I hope he will not wait until I drain the glass dry. I put it to my lips to take the first sip and he turns to draw the curtains. "Please, Father," I say.

"Can I leave them open? The moon is full tonight and I can see it from my bed."

"Of course." He stops at my door. As he gazes at me I see the worry in his eyes. "Good night, my son."

As soon as I hear his footsteps down the stairs, I leap from my bed and lock the door. Then I pull the curtains even wider. The moon is cold and beautiful. She will light my way tonight.

As the minutes grow into hours I feel the press of that other me eager to be free. I am so tired I can hardly fight him, but fight him I will. At moments my eyes almost close and I can feel him spring forward. I have to leap to my feet and cry out.

"NO!"

I will only let him out when I am ready.

The time drags on and on. I plan to wait until midnight, the witching hour. I have never been so bold before as to go out at this hour. But midnight is HIS time.

I hear the clock in the hall. I count its chimes – and there are twelve. Now, I think. *Now*.

I feel him rise within me, a child struggling to be born. Slow at first, coming from a place so deep he has to fight his way up, like a monster appearing from a dark lake. A hidden monster who sends water gushing, whose roars make the ground tremble.

He rises from my very soul.

It is a struggle to hold onto myself. I must keep from losing this part of me, this part that has the good in him, to share my body with this other me. But I will not let go.

At last he is here. I feel him as he squeezes in beside me, like a twin in the womb, like another body in a coffin. But I will not let go. I cling on.

So it is done.

I am on my knees, dragging a trunk out from under my bed. A brown leather trunk I have not opened in many years. I had forgotten it was even there. I take out trousers, old trousers I have grown out of, and a shirt too. It looks worn and old yet when I slip into these clothes they fit, and I feel that my body belongs in them. Shoes too, shoes I remember from many years ago. Yet they too fit onto my feet. I don't even question why that is. In these clothes more of me slinks back into the dark shadows of myself.

Now, the night must begin. I don't have to think about the path I must take. I know it by heart, because HE knows it. From my balcony I climb down to the ground. I am not afraid of the long drop onto the grass below. I have made it so often. When did I become so agile, so fearless and fleet? I hurry across the garden, invisible to any eyes, and take the narrow path that leads to the back alley. Everywhere is deserted and still, but as I come out into the street, I hear a carriage somewhere close by. I press myself into a wall, but the carriage rumbles past without anyone seeing me. Then I run again, fast.

Edinburgh Castle looms in the distance, its walls and turrets a darker line against the night sky. The moon drapes it in a silver shroud. I am headed for the Old Town. It pulls me to it. I belong there. As I near the old cobbled streets and closes I feel a change pulse within me. A gush of pleasure and excitement. It is HIM. He is becoming stronger, longing to be out, to be alone, desperate for his freedom. He wants to be rid of me. But I have to be the master tonight.

I come to a narrow close where damp steps rise to the dark street above. I begin to climb. I hear faint fiddle music and singing from a tavern. There will be people there, not yet aware of my approach. I crouch down as I pass the window because I must not be seen, not yet, not until I am ready.

For a short moment I am sure they will catch me. A man comes to the door of the tavern. The light from inside spills onto the cobbles. I try to melt into the wall. I must be seen. But not now. This is not the witness I need.

"Come and see this." The man calls back to someone inside the tavern. "Aye, you have to see this."

I cannot move. If I do I will have to pass right by him. He is sure to see the movement ... or has he seen me already? I close my eyes and wait.

I hear another man join him. "What's that?" he asks. His voice slurs and sloshes with too much beer.

"The moon." The first man's voice slurs too. "Izza beautiful full moon."

The other man laughs. I am so relieved I almost join him. I open my eyes as the second man drags his drunken friend back inside. The tavern door swings shut before I move on.

On the street I stay close to the wall. I seem to know where I am headed. Of course I know. Because HE knows and I am HE.

There is wickedness in him, and I feel it grow and pulse within me. That is not me, I think, surely that is not me. I stifle it, shake the evil away and head along the Royal Mile.

How do I begin? My plan is to be seen, I must be seen, but seen at the right time and by the right people. People the policemen will believe.

They must all know I am the one, the Beast they all fear, so the innocent boy can go free.

And in that moment I am no longer me. I feel as if I am a passenger in a carriage. I am trapped inside, and my eyes are like two glass windows. I am watching all that is going on from behind them. I am not the only passenger, but he has the reins of the horses now. He is the driver. I struggle, but with my tiredness and my fear he has gained strength. He is out. I am no longer the master.

He presses his face against a window. Inside I see a woman sewing in the light of a candle. I see a baby in a crib by her side. Now and then she rocks it with her foot. My face, HIS face, moves closer until I can feel the cold glass against my brow. For a moment I fear we have the power to melt inside the room. He raises a hand and touches the glass, and I see that it is no longer my hand. It is crooked and clawed. How and when did my hand change to this? He taps on the glass and the woman looks up at the sound. Her mouth forms a silent O, her eyes grow wide and, a moment later, she screams.

"It's him!"

He leaps back and lets out a laugh, a laugh of joy in the woman's fear. He laughs and laughs like some lunatic from the madhouse. I cannot stop him. The baby cries in alarm. The woman's screams grow more and more frantic. Figures appear from doorways, men and women. The cry goes up.

"The Bogeyman is back!"

"The Beast is among us!"

And the chase is on.

- 14 -

Hunted

I'm afraid. Never have I been so afraid, yet I can feel too the excitement he feels, as the thrill of the chase thunders along my veins. Alive, that is how I feel. I hear the crowd as it gathers behind us, but he, my other self, he knows these wynds and closes. I let him lead the way. I hear a roar behind me.

"Let me get him!" a voice bellows. "I will make him pay for what he did to Rolf."

Could this be the Big George Mary spoke of? As fierce as a lion, she said, and now he's an angry lion. A dangerous beast. Yet I am HIM, a part of me is HIM, and also a beast, and he is not afraid. He wants to turn and face him. He wants to yell, defiant, "Make me pay then, if you can!"

Then I hear a shout behind me. "Ah, the police are here! Come on, boys!"

So a constable has joined the chase, maybe more than one. I am glad. This is what I want. A policeman will make a better witness than the ruffians of the Old Town.

Never have I been so bold. I feel as if I am travelling inside another. He is carrying me along, this other me, in a carriage he is driving. I let him lead, but every second I feel him grow stronger and I must fight to stay alert and keep some kind of control of myself and him. Now, he is clambering over a wall. He leaps down onto mossy ground and we are in a graveyard. Edinburgh is full of graveyards, and people respect the dead that lie there. But the angry mob behind me will respect nothing. They will surge past headstones, and trample over graves to get at me.

I push my way past thorny bushes, keeping low to the ground, but then a stone angel looms through the trees and makes me jump. For a moment she seems alive. Her white face scares me, and her mouth is open, as if she is about to speak. Her pointing finger seems to be telling me to leave this holy place. Behind her, I can see men scaling the walls. The constable seems to be leading them now. They will be upon us soon, yet I cannot move.

"Look. He's here!"

The crowd is pointing at us. I see a mountain of a man crash to the ground. He roars. "He is mine!" I am sure this is Big George, seeking revenge for the killing of his dog. It must be him.

"We have to get away," I say. I move at last, but I have cost us time.

"We will," the other me replies.

We begin to run again. We leap across graves and over tombstones, dash behind trees and then scramble over another high stone wall. Behind us, they are closing in. We grab at a lamp-post, and climb it like a monkey climbing a tree. At the top we hang on and spin around as we look for a place to leap to. There is nowhere apart from the roof of a nearby building, but it is too far away. I am sure it is too far, we will never make it. I am sure we will never make it.

Why is he not as afraid as I am? And the answer comes to me – he is never afraid, or ashamed of anything he has done. He is me without fear and without conscience. He throws himself forward and we are flying. I hold my breath. My fear touches him, and for a moment I feel his confidence slip. We grab at the roof but the tiles are slippery. Our hands slither, scratch to try to get a hold, but in spite of my efforts we begin to slide down.

At the last moment we pull ourselves up. We press ourselves behind a chimney wall. From here we can see the men rush onto the narrow street below. They stop. They look all around.

"Where's he gone?" one asks.

"He can't just have disappeared."

I hold my breath, sure that at any moment they will look up and see us.

Big George roars again. "Where are you!"

His voice is so fierce that I jump and a loose slate clatters down. The noise is like the rattle of thunder. I watch the tile teeter on the edge of the roof. I pray it stays there. But a moment later it plummets to the ground.

Big George looks up. "There!" He points at me – I am a dark shape, clear against the moon. Bent and twisted, I must look like a horror in the sky.

They can all see us now.

One of the men pulls at the constable's sleeve. "That is the Beast. The real Beast."

And the constable responds. "It is indeed."

And, once more, the cry goes up. "Let's get him this time."

- 15 -

Strange Meeting

Where did I find the speed, the energy to move like this? And where did my daring come from? I am not even afraid.

I balance on the roof and walk to the edge, while the men screech and yell below me. Then I leap from one roof to the other. The men follow my progress, eager to see where I will go next. I take them by surprise as I break into a run and then I am leaping, flying like some wild bird from one roof to another. My heart is in my mouth – I am sure I won't make it this time. But HE is never afraid, this other me. He knows he can do it, and a second later I land on steady feet, and I am balancing high above the street. I can hear the shouts and yells of the men below, still giving chase. They have lost sight of us for the moment, but that won't last for long.

Where to go now?

I need not worry. He knows. He crouches down and crawls to the end of the old building then he clambers down the crow steps. I cannot look. If we fall ... but we do not fall. He is as sure on his feet as any animal. He slithers down a drainpipe on the other side of the building, away from the mob that is chasing us, and he leaps to the ground.

We cackle with glee, both of us, and I laugh as loud as he does, because we are like wild animals who have tricked our hunters again and got away. I feel the urge that is in him to turn and confront them, but I am the one who must be strong. I know we are running for home now. And I am glad. This is all I wanted. The constables have seen us, and so have many others. There have been enough witnesses now to make the police reconsider the innocent boy's guilt. We are no longer a shadow in the darkness. We have shown our face.

The cries sound distant now, and they are moving further away with each moment. They have lost us. For an instant I stop and look behind me. The streets are empty. All is quiet. Keep running, I tell myself. Keep running for home.

I turn a corner, and almost knock over a slight girl with her head covered in a shawl. I scramble back against a wall, and the girl wobbles but does not fall. The shawl slips off her head and I see her face.

I stare at her. She stares back at me. I am sure my heart stops beating as I wait for her to call my name. She looks ready to scream, and her mouth trembles as if the sound is trapped by fear ...

Mary. I want to say her name, but I dare not.

She steps back and holds out her hand with the palm towards me, as if to keep me distant from her.

"*I won't harm you, Mary. I could never harm you.*"

This is what I mean to say. Instead, I hear only a growl, a sound that comes from deep within me. It scares me, and it terrifies Mary. I see the scream catch in her throat. And I feel a change come over me. A change I cannot control. He is growing stronger. I have to force my hands to stay by my side. My fingers stretch out with a life of their own, and I am looking at Mary's smooth white neck and I can see these crooked fingers around that neck. What am I thinking?

No!

What is he thinking?

This is not me! I could never harm sweet Mary. I shake the awful thought away and rip my gaze from the flesh of her neck. I force HIM down, like the mad dog he is. I take another step back. I can hear again the cries of the hunters. They have turned and are heading this way. Mary hears them too. I stare at her, and my eyes plead for her to forgive me and remain silent.

Mary stares back at me. It's as if she sees the changes in me. Her brow crumples and she looks puzzled now. Now that she sees me, she knows who I am. She must. It's as if she is seeing something inside me that she recognises and that something is me. Yet she still says nothing.

Mary steps back, and I see a strange creature reflected in the window behind her. A creature bent low like an animal, with long arms dangling on the ground, and fingers scraping on the cobbles. And his face. Oh such a face, twisted and ugly.

Who is this?

And, in the same moment I ask the question, I answer it.

It is me.

Or the me I become on these night crawls in the city. It's as if all the evil that is within me rises to the surface and I, the real me, am pushed down into the darkness. No wonder Mary is afraid.

This cannot happen again.

I cannot let this happen again.

In despair I cover my face, and my hands rasp like claws on my skin.

I must run, before Mary realises it is me. Before HE, the other one, becomes more powerful again and this time I may not be able to stop him hurting her.

I take a step into the darkness, and I am gone.

A moment later Mary screams. I hear the shouts of the mob coming closer. The men will find her. But they must not find me.

- 16 -

Home

I am in my own bed. I am home. But I have no memory of how I got here. I close my eyes, and with no need of any tonic, I sleep.

The noise of my mother beating at the door brings me awake.

"Harry! Harry!" she calls.

I stumble from my bed, groggy, and open the door. She flies in and throws her arms around me. It's as if she has not seen me in months.

"Harry, I wish you would not lock yourself in. I was so afraid. We have been pounding on your door all morning. No one could wake you."

"I promise I will not lock my door in London, Mother," I tell her and I know that this is true.

I see the relief sweep over her at my words. "But you slept, my love, and for that I am so glad. Your father's sleeping tonic is a powerful one."

My eyes dart to the glass beside my bed, still full. I hope she does not see it. "It is excellent," I say, and I turn her to the door. "But I could sleep more, Mother."

"Oh yes, sleep some more, my boy. But do not lock the door this time."

After she has gone, I pour the contents of the glass onto the grass below my terrace. And I sleep again.

☾

It is late afternoon when at last I wake. The long shadows are at my window and the sky is dark. I dress and take the back staircase that leads to the kitchen. I have a great fear eating at me – the fear that Mary knew me, that she saw the truth. That constables are waiting to arrest me. I remember the way she stared at me last night, her puzzled look as if there was something about me she did not understand. Did it become clear to her? Who I must be? Who *he* must be? Has dear Mary gone to the police to expose me, to expose my secret?

The kitchen is buzzing with noise and heat. They are preparing dinner. I can hear Mrs Kerr, and the boy who delivers our meat, but above them all, I hear Mary.

"Tell me what you saw, Mary," the butcher boy is asking.

"She's told this story a dozen times," Mrs Kerr says. "We're all fed up with it."

"But I've not heard it, Mrs Kerr," the butcher boy says. "Go on, Mary, please."

Mary is only too pleased to go on. She is not fed up with her story.

"I was on my way here this morning," she starts. "I was coming early because there are so many trunks still to be packed, and he" – at this she hesitates – "or it, for it was only half human, I tell you, it came leaping out of the mist … I almost tumbled head over heels down the street! The fog seemed to cover him like a shroud. He looked like some bent and twisted ghost."

"Oh Mary!" Mrs Kerr scolds her. "Why do you have to embroider your stories like this?"

"I'm only telling the truth, Mrs Kerr. I did think he was a ghost," Mary declares. "One minute there was nothing there and the next he appears in a cloak of fog. Hands scraping the ground, black eyes just staring at me."

"Why didn't you run?" the butcher boy asks.

"I couldn't move, honest I couldn't," she says. "My feet were bolted to the ground. I always thought if I saw the creature I would be so brave. I'd fling my basket at him, leap on his back and hold him until help came. But in that moment I learned what a coward I am. I couldn't move. I couldn't take my eyes from him. And he could not take his eyes from me. And there was something in those eyes …" Mary stops.

I hold my breath.

What is she going to say next?

"Something I still cannot understand," Mary goes on. "I was sure he wanted to leap at me, and grab me, put those clawed hands around my throat and choke the life out of me ... and yet, there was something holding him back. That something seemed to be growing stronger ..." She pauses again before she adds, "I feel I should know what it is."

I cannot bear the suspense. I imagine her thinking back to that moment, remembering every detail. Now, at last, she will realise who she was looking at. Not a monster at all ... but me.

And then my secret will be out.

A shout rings out – "Who's there?"

Mrs Kerr pulls the kitchen door wide and finds me on the other side. "Oh, master Harry," she cries. "You shouldn't be listening to this." She turns to Mary. "You and your wild stories."

"No, no, please, I want to listen." I step into the kitchen and, for all it is the last thing I want to do, I must face Mary.

She stares at me for a long moment. I stare back. I wait. I need to hear whatever she says with honour.

"Go on, Mary. You were saying." I dare myself to say it out loud. "There was something you feel you should know?"

She still looks. Does she see the monster in me? The silence between us seems to last for ever.

I believe that the thought does come into her mind – the thought that I was the creature she saw in the night. But it is so ridiculous she can't believe it. She shakes her head and smiles.

"It was only a silly thought, sir," she says, "but in that moment I thought maybe this beast isn't all bad. That there might be a part of him that is good and true. He had the chance to kill me, to leave me dead in the street, yet he did not raise a hand to hurt me ..."

And so Mary finishes.

Mrs Kerr gives her arm a soft pat. "I am glad he did not, Mary. For all you're a chatterbox, I am very fond of you."

Mary laughs. "So am I, or I would not be here to tell my story. And it is a story I will tell my children and my grandchildren."

"I am sure you will." Mrs Kerr laughs with her. "Again, and again, and again."

I am safe.

The butcher boy has been hanging on Mary's every word too. "Wait till I tell my master," he says. And with that, he runs from the kitchen, eager to be off.

Mrs Kerr bustles over to her stove. "Sit down, young master," she says to me. "I have some hot broth for you. And you, Mary, get on with your work now – there's pots in the sink to scrub and those trunks won't pack themselves."

"I'm glad you are safe too, Mary," I tell her.

She gives a little bow and smiles. "Thank you, sir."

"You take care on those dark streets," I add. I don't want her to go just yet.

"Oh I will, but there is no danger there now, sir."

"Now?" I ask.

"The Beast is dead." She says it just like that.

- 17 -

The Beast Is Dead

The Beast is dead? Have I heard Mary right?

Mrs Kerr turns from the stove. "How is it you manage to get news before anyone else, Mary?" she asks, but she does not require nor expect an answer.

"Please, tell us what you mean, Mary," I demand. "Are they sure?" I won't let it go – I must know all.

"The men chasing him heard an awful scream at the mouth of one of the old sewers. When they got there they found his shirt, all torn and bloody, as if it had been ripped off him. But there was no sign of the creature. The men searched everywhere but they saw and heard nothing. And that's when they knew he must have slipped on the raw sewage. It's almost ankle deep there." Mary's pretty face screws up in disgust. "There's nothing to hold onto there. And, oh, even for a beast like him – what a terrible way to die."

"And his body?"

"My father says it might never be found. Nothing that goes in the sewers ever comes out alive. He's dead for sure." Mary shrugs. "The rats will make a feast of him."

Mrs Kerr tuts. "Oh Mary!"

"Well, rats have to eat too, Mrs Kerr," Mary says, and her smile is cheeky as she bangs the pots in the sink.

As she speaks, my memory of the night rushes into my mind. I re-live every moment as I sit at the table. I do not touch my bowl of broth.

☽

After I had left Mary the night before, I heard the mob coming closer. The fear hit me that perhaps I could not outrun them, that they would catch me and the evil part of me would disappear. Then I would be left to face them alone. But perhaps that was not my true fear, for I knew that I deserved any punishment the mob might hand out to me. My fear was the pain and shame I would cause my dear mother and father. Was that what gave me the speed to run on? Was that why I headed for the sewer?

I knew I must finish this once and for all.

There had to be a way to make the world believe this monster was dead.

But he knew what I meant to do and he fought me, trying to make me stop, to make me run for home. He wanted to live as much as I wanted him to die. The sewer would end it, one way or another. As I ran down an alley I stumbled into a pile of wooden crates. I did not stop, but the nails in the rough wood caught on my shirt. In my hurry to escape, I tugged the shirt from my body and left it.

Almost every sound around me faded away. I heard only my ragged breath coming in short gasps. That and the howls of the mob behind me.

The stink was disgusting. I was standing in filth up to my ankles and for a moment I began to slip and slide and there was nothing to hold on to. I was terrified that I would disappear into that black hole and never be found. I let out a yell of real terror, afraid for my life.

"What was that?" someone shouted.

"What's happened?"

The mob came running, but I did not wait. I pulled off my trousers and my shoes and watched them slide over the muck and the filth and down into the darkness. Then I was sprinting naked for home. I prayed they would fall for my trick.

It would appear from Mary's story that they had.

I had washed the stinking filth from myself in the fountain in our garden.

Yet, I had remembered nothing, until I listened to Mary tell her story. All of this had been blotted from my mind.

Mrs Kerr shakes my arm. "You look pale, sir," she says. "And so quiet. Are you well? You went into a wee dwam there."

I smile. "I am better than I ever was, Mrs Kerr. Mary's story has lifted my spirits." Yet there is still one question I must ask. "And what of the boy who was arrested?"

"That is the good news, sir." Mary is all smiles. "The boy is to be released," she says. "Too many saw the Beast last night for the boy to be guilty."

Her words are all I want to hear. "I am so glad," I say.

Mrs Kerr squeezes my arm. "You are a kind boy to worry about a poor soul like him."

But Mary looks at me, puzzled by my concern.

- 18 -

Release

My father tells me the same story at dinner that night. About the chase, about the torn and bloody shirt, and about the many witnesses who had seen the Beast. Mrs Kerr is right to wonder, I think. How does Mary get all this information?

"So it seems it is over," my father finishes, and he lifts his wine glass. "This creature is gone, for ever we hope."

"And the boy?" I ask.

"I have been to the prison and examined the boy again, and I signed for his release. He will soon be free."

I have done what I had to do, but the boy's future still feels so bleak. "Will he go back to the underground tunnels again, Father?" I ask. "To live in that hellish place under our city?"

"No," my father says, and I hear a satisfied note in his voice. "I have arranged for him to train as a blacksmith outside the city. I think, I hope, his life will be better now. He has a second chance. A chance to have a different life, to become a different person."

A different person.

I too have a second chance. I too will be a different person.

It is not too late for me to change. I am only a boy. I am young. I can put this evil creature back in the bottle, and put the stopper on so he goes back into the darkness. In truth, I can find it in my heart to pity him. Yet he must go. I buried him before and forgot him. I can do so again. This time, I will bury him so deep he will never escape. I will lock him so deep inside myself that I will forget he ever existed, and I will never let him out again.

I will make my father proud. And I will be
what I have always wanted to be – a doctor.

Doctor Henry Jekyll.

About *The Evil Within*

I always do an April Fool every year. Once I said that Steven Spielberg was just off the phone wanting to make my Nemesis series into a blockbuster movie. And, to my surprise, almost everyone believed me. So a couple of years ago on the 1st of April I said I'd been asked to write a book about young Henry Jekyll and, once again, not only did my friends believe me, they thought it was a great idea too. Then my agent told me she thought so as well, and I realised the idea had been in my head for a long time.

I love Robert Louis Stevenson, and have always felt a connection with him. And I particularly love the story of Jekyll and Hyde. Is it something in my psyche? I've always been fascinated by doubles and doppelgängers. I love them and they scare me too. I've even written a book about a doppelgänger, based on a nightmare I had when I was a child that I have never forgotten.

So, *The Evil Within* was both a labour of love and something that felt irresistible, unavoidable, inevitable. The book and its story were haunting me before I ever set pen to paper. I can only hope that my story does justice to its original source – *The Strange Case of Dr Jekyll and Mr Hyde* – and to my inspiration, the great Scottish novelist, poet and man of letters, Robert Louis Stevenson.

The idea for *Dr Jekyll and Mr Hyde* came to Stevenson in a fever dream in 1886 when he was just 36. "I was dreaming a fine bogey tale," he told his wife Fanny when she woke him from his dreadful nightmare. Stevenson burned the first draft of *Jekyll and Hyde* and started again from scratch after Fanny read it and hated it. The story goes that Stevenson wrote his second draft in three days. And – even though I'm a wee bit older than 36 now! – that was the challenge I set myself. I set aside those three days and I just wrote and wrote and wrote. And that was *The Evil Within* finished, with time to spare! But, you know, I feel I wasn't so much writing it as copying it down from the voice in my head narrating it to me. Who knows, perhaps the voice was that of Robert Louis Stevenson, my other self, helping me along.

The idea of Jekyll and Hyde still exerts a strong hold on our imaginations. In part, this is thanks to Stevenson's brilliant writing, bringing to life the idea that good and evil can be present in the same body and mind. This double edge to our nature is something that has always fascinated me and it sent shivers down my spine to imagine the childhood of young Harry Jekyll. I hope it thrills you too, and that one day you will read Stevenson's incredible novella.

Catherine MacPhail
Edinburgh, 2017

If *The Evil Within* sent a chill down your spine, then why not try our super-readable edition of Stevenson's original 'shilling shocker'?

Published in a unique, dyslexia-friendly format in August 2017

Our books are tested
for children and young people by
children and young people.

Thanks to everyone who consulted on
a manuscript for their time and effort in
helping us to make our books better
for our readers.